Let's go to the Swings

Level 2E

D1445139

Written by Lucy George
Illustrated by Andrew Geeson
Reading Consultant: Betty Franchi

About Phonics

Spoken English uses more than 40 speech sounds. Each sound is called a *phoneme*. Some phonemes relate to a single letter (d-o-g) and others to combinations of letters (sh-ar-p). When a phoneme is written down, it is called a *grapheme*. Teaching these sounds, matching them to their written form, and sounding out words for reading is the basis of phonics.

Early phonics instruction gives children the tools to sound out, blend, and say the words without having to rely on memory or guesswork. This instruction gives children the confidence and ability to read unfamiliar words, helping them progress toward independent reading.

About the Consultant

Betty Franchi is an American educator with a Bachelor's Degree in Elementary and Middle Education as well as a Master's Degree in Special Education. Betty holds a National Boards for Professional Teaching Standards certification. Throughout her 24 years as a teacher, she has studied and developed an expertise in Phonetic Awareness and has implemented phonetic strategies, teaching many young children to read, including students with special needs.

Reading tips

 This book focuses on the *ng* sound as in ring.

Tricky and/or new words in this book

Any words in bold may have unusual spellings
or are new and have not yet been introduced.

Tricky and/or new words in this book

**go the be they play park
to bees she where were**

Extra ways to have fun with this book

After the readers have finished the story, ask them
questions about what they have just read.

What was the name of the puppy in the story?
What did Anna and Kit play on in the park?

Explain that the two letters *ng* make one sound.
Think of other words that use the *ng* sound,
such as *sting* and *sing*.

I like creeping
through long, tall grass.
Sometimes I think
I am a tiger!

A Pronunciation Guide

This grid highlights the sounds used in the story and offers a guide on how to say them.

s as in sat	a as in ant	t as in tin	p as in pig	i as in ink
n as in net	c as in cat	e as in egg	h as in hen	r as in rat
m as in mug	d as in dog	g as in get	o as in ox	u as in up
l as in log	f as in fan	b as in bag	j as in jug	v as in van
w as in wet	z as in zip	y as in yet	k as in kit	qu as in quick
x as in box	ff as in off	ll as in ball	ss as in kiss	zz as in buzz
ck as in duck	pp as in puppy	nn as in bunny	rr as in arrow	gg as in egg
dd as in daddy	bb as in chubby	tt as in attic	sh as in shop	ch as in chip
th as in them	th as in thin	ng as in sing		

Be careful not to add an /uh/ sound to /s/, /t/, /p/, /c/, /h/, /r/, /m/, /d/, /g/, /l/, /f/ and /b/. For example, say /ff/ not /fuh/ and /sss/ not /suh/.

Anna and Kit **go to the** swings.
Kit cannot **be** gone long.

Anna tells Kit to run. "Hurry!"
Anna is bossy.

Kit brings her dog, Jim.
Jim is a puppy.

They get to the swings
and Jim zips off.

Anna and Kit **play** on all the things in the **park**.

Jim runs after a fox.
The fox is very quick.

Anna and Kit hang
on the bars.

Jim runs after the **bees**.
The bees buzz.

Anna and Kit go up and down.

Jim runs after a kitten.
The kitten is chubby.

Anna and Kit swing on the swings and sing a song.

"The big swing is the best!"

Kit swings up and up.
"I am the king!" **she** sings.

Where is Jim?

Jim runs after baby Bobby.
Kit yells at Jim to stop.

Anna and Kit run back. Jim runs along. The swings **were** fun.

OVER 48 TITLES IN SIX LEVELS
Betty Franchi recommends...

Some titles from Level 1

I love reading phonics — **Bad Rat**	I love reading phonics — **The Best Gift**	I love reading phonics — **Clint and Grant Play I-Spy**	I love reading phonics — **Bret and Grandma's Trip!**
978 1 84898 747 0	978 1 84898 750 0	978 1 84898 752 4	978 1 84898 751 7

Other titles to enjoy from Level 2

I love reading phonics — **Chuck and Duck**	I love reading phonics — **Wish Fish**	I love reading phonics — **Kyle in Trouble**
978 1 84898 756 2	978 1 84898 755 5	978 1 84898 762 3

Some titles from Level 3

I love reading phonics — **Bart's Go-Cart**	I love reading phonics — **Queen Ella's Feet**	I love reading phonics — **Puff Flies**	I love reading phonics — **The Pop Duet**
978 1 84898 768 5	978 1 84898 764 7	978 1 84898 765 4	978 1 84898 767 8

An Hachette Company
First Published in the United States by TickTock, an imprint of Octopus Publishing Group.
www.octopusbooksusa.com

Copyright © Octopus Publishing Group Ltd 2013

Distributed in the US by
Hachette Book Group USA
237 Park Avenue, New York NY 10017, USA

Distributed in Canada by
Canadian Manda Group
165 Dufferin Street, Toronto, Ontario, Canada M6K 3H6

ISBN 978 1 84898 759 3

Printed and bound in China
10 9 8 7 6 5 4 3 2 1

All rights reserved. No part of this work may be reproduced or utilized in any form or by any means,
electronic or mechanical, including photocopying, recording or by any information storage and retrieval system,
without the prior written permission of the publisher.